Magic Puppy

*To Scarlet—sweet spotty girl with
the funny Dally grin*

GROSSET & DUNLAP
Published by the Penguin Group
Penguin Group (USA) Inc., 375 Hudson Street,
New York, New York 10014, USA
Penguin Group (Canada), 90 Eglinton Avenue East, Suite 700,
Toronto, Ontario M4P 2Y3, Canada
(a division of Pearson Penguin Canada Inc.)
Penguin Books Ltd., 80 Strand, London WC2R 0RL, England
Penguin Group Ireland, 25 St. Stephen's Green, Dublin 2, Ireland
(a division of Penguin Books Ltd.)
Penguin Group (Australia), 250 Camberwell Road,
Camberwell, Victoria 3124, Australia
(a division of Pearson Australia Group Pty. Ltd.)
Penguin Books India Pvt. Ltd., 11 Community Centre, Panchsheel Park,
New Delhi—110 017, India
Penguin Group (NZ), 67 Apollo Drive, Rosedale, North Shore 0632, New Zealand
(a division of Pearson New Zealand Ltd.)
Penguin Books (South Africa) (Pty.) Ltd., 24 Sturdee Avenue,
Rosebank, Johannesburg 2196, South Africa

Penguin Books Ltd., Registered Offices:
80 Strand, London WC2R 0RL, England

Text copyright © 2008 Sue Bentley. Illustrations copyright © 2008 Angela Swan. Cover illustration copyright © 2008 Andrew Farley. First printed in Great Britain in 2008 by Penguin Books Ltd. First published in the United States in 2010 by Grosset & Dunlap, a division of Penguin Young Readers Group, 345 Hudson Street, New York, New York 10014. GROSSET & DUNLAP is a trademark of Penguin Group (USA) Inc. Printed in the U.S.A.

Library of Congress Cataloging-in-Publication Data is available.

ISBN 978-0-448-45066-7   10 9 8 7 6 5 4 3 2

Magic Puppy

Twirling Tails

SUE BENTLEY

Illustrated by Angela Swan

Grosset & Dunlap
An Imprint of Penguin Group (USA) Inc.

Prologue

As a terrifying howl rose into the night air, the young, silver-gray wolf froze.

"Shadow!" Storm gasped. The evil lone wolf who had attacked the Moon-claw pack was very close.

Storm scanned the snow-covered hillside with scared, midnight blue eyes. He should have known it was dangerous to come back home. He needed to act quickly.

Sparks crackled in the young wolf's thick fur and there was a flash of bright gold light. Where Storm had stood, there now crouched a tiny light brown puppy with a stocky body and shaggy fur.

Storm's little puppy heart beat fast as he leaped forward and ran across the frozen ground. He hoped this disguise would protect him until he found somewhere to hide.

There were some snow-covered bushes nearby. Storm wriggled under a low branch and lay there trembling. A rustling sound came from farther back in the bushes and icy snow fell onto the tiny puppy. As the branches parted to reveal the shape of a large wolf, Storm froze and his midnight blue eyes widened in terror. Shadow had found him!

"I am glad to see you, my son. But it is not safe for you to be here," the wolf rumbled softly.

"Mother!" Storm yipped in relief. His whole body wriggled and he wagged his sturdy little tail as he squirmed toward her.

Canista reached out one huge paw and pulled her disguised cub close. She whined fondly as she licked his little square muzzle and low-set ears, but her gold eyes filled with concern.

"You cannot stay. You are the only cub left in the Moon-claw pack. Shadow wants to be leader, but the others have scattered and will not follow him while you live."

Storm growled softly and his midnight blue eyes glowed with fury as he thought of the fierce wolf who had killed his father and three litter brothers.

"I am tired of hiding. I will fight Shadow now!" he yapped.

Canista shook her head slowly. "Bravely said. But Shadow is too strong for you and I am still too weak from his poisoned bite to help you. Go back to the other world. Return when you are stronger and wiser and lead the Moon-claw pack." As she stopped speaking, her gentle eyes clouded with pain.

Storm whined softly. He leaned close and huffed out a warm breath of shimmering gold sparks. They swirled around Canista's paw like golden smoke before disappearing into her gray fur.

Canista gave a long sigh. "Thank you, Storm. The pain is lessening."

But before Storm could finish healing

her wound, another deafening howl rang out. The sound of mighty paws thudding on the frozen ground came closer.

"Shadow knows you are here! Go now. Save yourself," Canista urged.

Bright gold sparks bloomed in the tiny puppy's shaggy, light brown fur.

Storm whined softly as he felt the power building inside him. The glow of golden light around him grew brighter. And brighter . . .

Chapter
ONE

Kirsten Blake twirled her baton high into the air as she marched around the gym. She caught the baton perfectly without missing a beat of her routine.

"Yes," she whispered to herself, delighted that all her practice was beginning to pay off.

Swinging her arms, Kirsten kept perfect time with the other Limelight Majorettes as they wheeled and interwove in time to the music.

"Shoulders back, heads up. Looking

good!" Molly the trainer cried. Kirsten's blond hair was tied back and she wore shorts and a blue T-shirt with "LM" in glittery letters on the front.

As the music ended, all the majorettes stopped at exactly the same moment.

"Good job, everyone," Molly praised. "Take a break now. After you get yourselves a drink, can we all gather together, please? I want to talk to you."

Kirsten wiped her face on a towel and then went to get a drink from the machine.

Molly was already there. She leaned down to take a can from the chute.

"You've really improved lately, Kirsten," she said smiling.

Kirsten felt a glow of pride. "Thanks. I love baton twirling. I even march all around the house doing it. Dad says it's a wonder I'm not twirling in my sleep!"

Molly laughed. "That would be one way to get more practice in. But I can't say I recommend it!"

The gym door opened and a girl

wearing jeans and a fleece sauntered in carrying a sports bag. She went over to a corner and dumped her bag.

It was Tracy Owen, Kirsten's best friend.

Kirsten and Tracy were in the same class at school and usually walked to majorette practice together. But tonight, Tracy had told Kirsten that she'd meet her there.

Kirsten noticed Molly looking across at Tracy. The trainer was shaking her head with annoyance.

Kirsten quickly got a second can from the machine and hurried straight over to Tracy. "Here you are. I got you this. Molly's on the warpath about you being late," she warned her. "Where have you been, anyway?"

"Thanks." Tracy took the drink and popped the tab. "Nowhere," she said in answer to Kirsten's question. "I don't know why Molly's in such a huff. There's not exactly much going on here."

"That's only because we're having a break, silly," Kirsten said, giving her a friendly dig. "We've all been practicing like maniacs. You should have seen me. I just did the most mega-high twirl *and* I managed to catch the baton!"

"Good for you," Tracy murmured without enthusiasm.

Kirsten's high spirits wavered a bit. Tracy seemed to be in a strange mood. She saw that Molly was coming over.

"Hello, Tracy," Molly said. "I expected

you to come straight over to me. Don't
you have something you want to say?"

Tracy flushed. "Um . . . I suppose so.
Sorry I'm a little late."

"You're over an hour late! And it's not
the first time. I think you owe me an
explanation," Molly said.

Tracy shuffled her feet and looked
at the floor. "I went to see one of my
classmates. She's . . . er . . . really sick.
We got talking and I didn't notice the
time."

Kirsten was puzzled. Why hadn't Tracy
told *her* that? And she couldn't think of
any girls in their class who were out sick.
She threw Tracy a questioning look, but
her friend didn't meet her eye.

Molly sighed. "We'll say no more
about it. But will you make sure that you
get here on time from now on?"

Tracy nodded.

"Good. Finish getting changed and
then come and sit with the others. I'm
about to make an announcement," Molly
said as she walked away.

"She's really bossy," Tracy grumbled, pulling on her sneakers. "I'm fed up with her ordering us all around like we're little kids."

"Well, she is the trainer. That's what they do," Kirsten said reasonably.

Tracy rolled her eyes. "Yeah, well. She should lighten up. So I was late. It's not a crime, is it?" She stomped moodily over to a pile of gym mats.

Kirsten followed her and they sat down to listen to Molly, who was already speaking.

". . . and as you know, the new shopping mall on Main Street is almost finished. In two weeks, it's going to be officially opened by the mayor. There'll be street performers, jugglers, and a fair

in the market square. And we've been asked to lead the Grand Parade. The Limelight Majorettes will be marching along to the music of a brass band!" Molly said with a smile.

"Wow! That's cool!" Kirsten said, as excited chatter broke out all around her and even Tracy looked impressed.

It was Kirsten's dream to perform with

the Limelight Majorettes, but only the
A team marched in public and went to
competitions. She and Tracy were still
on the B team.

Molly smiled around at all the eager
faces. "This is a great chance for us
to show everyone what we can do.
I want as many as possible of you to
take part. So I'm going to move
those of you who are ready onto the
A team.

". . . Annie and Rosa. And Jacqui
you'll all be moving up. And last but
not least . . . Kirsten, you'll be joining
the A team."

"Me? Yay! That's fantastic!" Kirsten
cried, delightedly bouncing up and
down on the springy gym mats.

Tracy sat there with her arms folded, saying nothing.

Kirsten's high spirits took a dive as she realized that her friend's name hadn't been called.

Molly clapped her hands. "Okay, everyone. Let's have another run-through."

As the others dispersed, Kirsten stood up and pulled Tracy to her feet.

"Molly, I think you've forgotten someone—Tracy!" she whispered urgently.

Molly shook her head. "I didn't forget. I'm just not sure that Tracy wants to give one hundred percent to the LMs right now. But I'd be happy to be proven wrong," she said more gently, giving Tracy a meaningful look before she walked away.

Tracy watched her go without speaking.

Kirsten looked at her friend. "Did you hear that? Molly more or less said that if you work really hard at practice now, you'll get onto the A team, too!" she said eagerly.

Tracy shrugged. "Who cares? Maybe Helena's right. Dressing up like a chocolate soldier is pretty stupid—" She stopped suddenly. "I'd better start work before Molly has a fit." Tracy went to join some girls who were doing warm-ups.

Kirsten frowned. Did Tracy mean Helena Simpson, the new girl in class? Helena was popular with everyone and gave noisy opinions about everything. Kirsten didn't think Tracy even knew her that well.

A suspicion came over her. What if Tracy had just been at Helena's house? But that couldn't be right because Tracy said her classmate had been sick and Helena had been fine at school earlier. Unless Tracy was lying . . .

Kirsten didn't want to believe it. She wandered miserably into the bathroom. There was no one else in there as she splashed her face at a sink. But as she looked back up into the mirrors, a dazzling flash of bright gold light lit up the whole room behind her.

"Oh!" Kirsten took a step backward, rubbing at her eyes. When her sight cleared, she turned to see a tiny puppy standing about a foot away on the tiled floor. It had light brown shaggy fur, a little square muzzle, and enormous midnight blue eyes.

"I need to hide. Can you help me?" it woofed.

Chapter
TWO

Kirsten's jaw dropped and she stared at the puppy in total amazement. She must be more upset by the idea of Tracy and Helena meeting behind her back than she thought. She'd actually just imagined that the puppy had spoken to her!

"Hello. Aren't you a little cutie? Where did you just come from?" she crooned, bending down to talk to it. She'd never seen a puppy with such bright blue eyes before.

The puppy pricked up its ears. It sat

down and put its head to one side. "I have come from far away. I am Storm of the Moon-claw pack. What is your name?"

"You really *can* talk!" Kirsten gasped, almost losing her balance and toppling

backward onto her behind. She just
managed to grab hold of a nearby sink and
steady herself before rising to her feet.

Kirsten felt like pinching herself to make
sure she wasn't dreaming. Talking puppies
didn't just appear out of thin air in gym
bathrooms. They only existed in fairy tales.

But Storm still sat there, looking up at her trustingly. The tiny puppy seemed to be waiting for her reply.

"I'm Kirsten. Kirsten Blake," she found herself saying. "I'm . . . er . . . one of the Limelight Majorettes. We practice here twice a week."

Storm dipped his head in a formal little bow. "I am honored to meet you, Kirsten."

"Um . . . me, too," Kirsten said. Her curiosity was starting to get the better of her shock. Despite its tiny size, the cute puppy didn't seem to be too scared of her.

"What was that you said about a . . . Moon-something?" she asked him.

Storm lifted his little head proudly.

"The Moon-claw pack. My mother and father were the leaders. But Shadow, an evil lone wolf, attacked us. Now my father and litter brothers are dead and my mother is wounded. Shadow wants to be leader now, but the other wolves will not follow him. They are waiting for me."

Kirsten frowned as she took this in. "But how can you lead a wolf pack? You're just a tiny pu–"

He stood up. Bright gold sparks bloomed in his shaggy, light brown fur and there was another dazzling flash of light.

Kirsten blinked hard as the light gradually faded. The tiny puppy was gone and in its place stood a majestic, young, silver-gray wolf with glowing midnight blue eyes. Its thick neck-ruff shimmered, as if it had been sprinkled all over with gold dust.

"Storm?" As Kirsten eyed the wolf's strong muscles, powerful, oversized paws, and long, sharp teeth, she started to back away.

"Yes, it is me, Kirsten. Do not be afraid. I will not harm you," Storm said in a deep, velvety growl.

Kirsten hardly had time to get used to seeing Storm as his amazing real self before there was a final burst of bright light and a fountain of gold sparks sprinkled down around her and fizzed out as they hit the floor tiles. Storm stood there once again as a tiny, helpless puppy.

"Wow!" she breathed in wonder. "That was incredible. No one would know that you're really a wolf in disguise."

"Shadow will know if he finds me," Storm woofed nervously. "Can you help me? I need to find somewhere safe to hide."

Kirsten could see that the puppy was beginning to tremble all over. She felt her heart melt. As his real self, Storm

was stunning, but as a cute, dewy-eyed, little puppy he was the most adorable thing Kirsten had ever seen.

She bent down and picked him up. As she stroked the fur on Storm's deep little chest, he reached up and licked her. His whiskery little muzzle brushed her chin.

"That really tickles!" Kirsten said, giggling and pulling back out of reach. "I've decided that you're coming home with me. Mom and Dad won't mind. We belong to Paws, an animal charity, and we're always taking care of cats and dogs until they can be adopted."

"I would like to live with you very much!" Storm yapped eagerly. His little mouth opened in a doggy grin, revealing his sharp, white teeth.

"I can't wait to show you to Tracy," Kirsten said, hoping that maybe this news would shake Tracy out of her odd mood and then their friendship could get back to normal. "She's my best friend. She's going to be so—" Kirsten began.

"No, Kirsten!" Storm reared up to look into her face, his sparkling blue eyes suddenly serious. "I am sorry, but you cannot tell anyone about me. Promise me that you will keep my secret."

Kirsten felt disappointed that she couldn't tell her friend the exciting news about Storm, but if it meant keeping Storm safe she decided she wouldn't say anything. Besides, Tracy didn't seem to be in the mood for sharing secrets right now.

"Okay, I promise. Cross my heart," she said.

As Storm relaxed against her again, Kirsten had a sudden thought. "There are tons of people in the gym. How am I going to smuggle you out of here without anyone noticing?"

Storm's teeth showed in another doggy grin. "Do not worry. I will use my magic, so that only you will be able to see and hear me."

"You can make yourself invisible? That's *so* cool!" Kirsten said. "Maybe you'd better do it now, before someone else comes in here."

Storm's midnight blue eyes glinted and a few tiny sparks flared in his light brown fur. "It is done."

"Really? Wow! Well, I'd better get back to practice now. Let's go." Kirsten put Storm down on the tiled floor and he trotted at her heels as she went to rejoin the others.

Kirsten felt really tense. Even though Storm had told her that he was invisible, she couldn't quite make herself believe

it and kept expecting someone to notice
him. But when no one did, Kirsten
relaxed and took her place in line.

As she began twirling her baton,
Kirsten's heart lifted at the thought of
the magical little friend who was sitting
watching and her worries about whether
Helena was trying to get friendly with
Tracy faded for the time being.

Chapter
THREE

"What an absolutely gorgeous puppy!" Kirsten's mom said. She bent down to stroke the tiny puppy's low-set ears. "I think he's a Border terrier. Imagine you just finding him wandering down the main road all by himself like that."

"Mmm. Weird, wasn't it?" Kirsten said vaguely.

"What did Tracy say? Didn't she want to take Storm home with her?" her mom asked.

"I didn't walk home with Tracy. She

rushed off the minute practice ended. I
guess she had to meet her mom from
work or something," Kirsten told her.

Mrs. Blake raised her eyebrows, but
didn't comment.

"Anyway, Storm's one lucky pup to
have found us, isn't he? He told me
that he—" Kirsten stopped quickly as
she realized that she would have to be a
lot more careful about keeping Storm's
secret. "I . . . um . . . mean, he obviously
needed a home. And I thought he could
stay with us," she finished quickly.

"Well, we're certainly used to looking
after strays." Her mom smiled and bent
down to pick Storm up. The little puppy
whined and began licking her all over
her face.

Mrs. Blake laughed. "Thanks, Storm, but I've already showered today! I like his name. It really suits him," she said to her daughter. "I'll call Paws and let them know that we've got a puppy that needs a permanent home. We'd better put a note by the newsstand, too, just in case an owner's looking for him."

"Good idea," Kirsten agreed, feeling confident that no one was going to be claiming this particular puppy. "And if no one comes for Storm, we could keep him forever, couldn't we?" she said in her best pleading voice.

Her mom frowned. "You know the rules, sweetie. We take care of animals until they can be adopted. If we kept every stray, we'd be overrun with cats and dogs."

"Okay," Kirsten sighed, knowing that she'd have to be satisfied with that for now, but she secretly promised herself to work hard to change her mom's mind. "I'll take Storm into the kitchen and get him some food. I bet he's really hungry."

"Food?" Storm barked eagerly, his ears

twitching. He started squirming to be let down.

Mrs. Blake smiled as she placed the wriggling little puppy back on the floor. "I could swear he understood every word you just said!"

Kirsten bit back a grin as she went out with Storm ambling after her. "If only Mom knew how right she was!" she whispered to him.

In the kitchen, Kirsten scooped canned dog food into a bowl and stood watching as Storm scarfed it down in about half a minute.

"Thank you. That was delicious," he woofed, licking his chops clean.

After she'd washed his bowl, Kirsten let Storm out for a short run in the garden and then got herself a drink and some cookies.

"Let's go to my room and I'll show you where you can sleep," she said, heading toward the stairs. On the way, Kirsten popped her head around the living room door and spoke to her mom and dad. "I'm going to finish my art homework and then get ready for bed. See you later."

"All right, sweetheart," her dad said.

In her bedroom, Kirsten spread an old blanket on her duvet and then lifted Storm onto it. "There you are. A cozy bed, especially for you."

With an eager little whine, Storm began sniffing around and scrabbling the blanket into messy folds. Once he was satisfied, he plunked down and rested his button-like black nose on his front paws.

"This is a good place. I feel safe here," he yawned.

"Glad you like it," Kirsten said. She smiled at the sleepy puppy, feeling a surge of affection for him. She took a folder and pencil case from her school bag. "We're studying Van Gogh in art. I'm making a copy of his painting of sunflowers with markers . . ."

But Storm wasn't listening. He sighed contentedly and moments later, tiny snores rose from his curled little form.

The next morning, Kirsten was almost ready to leave for school. She felt a bit nervous about seeing Tracy. This new

friendship with Helena was playing on
her mind and she wondered whether she
should talk to Tracy about it or not say
anything.

Kirsten sighed as she packed her folder
and the finished sunflower picture into
her shoulder bag. Storm sat on the front-
doormat watching her as she reached for
her coat.

"I hope you won't be too bored while

I'm away," Kirsten said as she fastened
the buttons. "I'll take you for a great long
walk as soon as I get back—promise!" she
said, smiling at him.

Storm jumped up and wagged his
sturdy little tail. "We can go for a walk
right now. I will come with you," he
woofed eagerly.

"I really wish you could, but we're not allowed to bring pets to school," Kirsten explained regretfully.

"But I am not a pet!" Storm yapped. "And no one will know that I am there."

Kirsten remembered that Storm could make himself invisible, but she was still unsure about having a lively puppy in the classroom. It could lead to all kinds of trouble.

"Well . . . okay, then. But you'll have to be extra careful to stay out of everyone's way," she decided. "Our teacher, Miss Strong, is really nice, but she's really strict."

Storm's eyes sparkled with triumph. He turned and began pawing the front door impatiently.

Kirsten laughed at his mischievousness. "Hey! Hang on, you! I think you should get in my shoulder bag. We have to cross some busy roads."

"Okay," Storm yapped. As soon as Kirsten opened her bag, he scrambled inside.

Kirsten said good-bye to her mom before they set off for Chaucer Crescent, where Tracy lived.

"Tracy's house is number thirty-seven," Kirsten told Storm as they walked along the sidewalk. "There she is now."

Tracy was just coming out of her house. A tall girl with long blond hair and a thin face was with her.

Kirsten recognized Helena Simpson. She stopped in dismay as her suspicions seemed to be confirmed. "Why is she picking up Tracy? Everyone knows that Tracy's *my* best friend!"

Chapter
FOUR

Kirsten and Storm waited for the two girls to reach them. "Hi, Tracy. Hi, Helena," Kirsten said, trying to sound a lot more cheerful than she felt.

"Hi, Kirsten," Helena replied.

"Helena just got here. She thought we could all walk to school together," Tracy said.

Kirsten shrugged. "Okay."

"How did it go at majorettes' practice last night? Did you do tons of prancing on tippy-toes?" Helena asked, smirking.

Kirsten was taken aback and took a moment to reply. "That's ballet. We do marching routines with twirling batons and stuff. It's more like cheerleading."

"Sounds okay. If you're about six years old!" Helena said, rolling her eyes as if she'd just made a clever joke.

Kirsten didn't laugh. "You can be any age over five. Some of the seniors are

eighteen. I like being a majorette. It's
fun."

"You like showing off, you mean!"
Helena crowed.

"No, I don't!" Kirsten felt her jaw
drop.

"Kirsten's not like that," Tracy
defended her.

"Whatever," Helena drawled. "Anyway,
last night I thought you said that baton
twirling and marching were pathetic."

Tracy looked uncomfortable. "You said
that. I only agreed with you because I
thought you were joking!"

"You were with Helena last night?"
Kirsten said to Tracy, trying to sound
casual.

Her friend nodded. "I went to help

Helena with her homework. I was going to tell you. But after Molly yelled at me for being late for practice, I didn't get around to it. You don't mind, do you?"

Kirsten did mind, but she didn't want to show it. She made herself shrug. "'Course not. Why should I?"

Tracy looked relieved. She smiled at Helena. "I told you Kirsten would be fine about it."

"Oh good," Helena said, smiling sweetly. "Then we can all be best friends, can't we?"

No we can't, Kirsten wanted to shout. She and Tracy had been best friends since forever. They didn't need anyone else.

As they all made their way to school, Kirsten slipped her hand into her shoulder bag and gently petted Storm's fuzzy little head, trying to ignore the horrible sinking feeling in her tummy. She was really glad that her new little friend would be with her all day.

Kirsten sat staring into space, gloomily

twiddling her thumbs. She was at her usual desk behind Tracy, near the back of the class. Helena sat a couple of desks away from them both, closer to the front.

Storm was off somewhere, sniffling around and exploring the classroom, invisible to everyone except Kirsten.

Miss Strong took attendance. She was small and very pretty, with stylish hair. She had lots of pairs of designer glasses. Today she wore narrow, purple ones.

"Here, Miss," Kirsten answered when her name was called out.

As Miss Strong put the class list away in her desk drawer, Kirsten caught sight of Storm.

The tiny puppy was just backing out of an open cabinet that he'd been

investigating. Storm saw Kirsten looking
at him. He gave an excited little woof
and almost fell over his own paws as he
came trotting toward her.

Storm plunked himself down at her
feet, his pink tongue lolling out. Despite

herself, Kirsten couldn't help smiling. "Having fun?" she whispered.

Storm nodded happily. "There are many wonderful smells in here."

Miss Strong's voice rang out again, almost making Kirsten jump.

"Okay, class. Can you get your art folders out, please?"

Kirsten fished her folder out of her bag. As she spread the contents onto her desk, Storm leaped up to sit beside her. His light brown fur was trailing tiny glimmering sparks.

Storm leaned forward curiously to see what Kirsten was doing. After quickly checking that no one was looking, she reached out to pet him. "I'm so glad that you're my friend," she whispered.

"Me too," Storm woofed softly.

As Kirsten sat back in her chair, something stung her below one eye. "Ow!" she cried in surprise as a tightly rolled paper pellet bounced down onto her desk.

Helena waved her ruler in the air, grinning triumphantly.

"That really hurt. It almost hit me in the eye!" Kirsten fumed.

Helena rolled her eyes. "*Some* people can't take a joke," she said under her breath.

Miss Strong looked up at them over the top of her glasses. "Kirsten? Helena? What's going on?" she demanded.

"Nothing, Miss," Kirsten said quickly, but the teacher had already noticed the ruler in Helena's hand. "Are you flicking things around, Helena? Do I have to ask you to come and sit at the front so I can keep an eye on you?"

"No way, Miss," Helena said, slapping the ruler onto her desk.

Miss Strong gave her a stern look. "I'm very glad to hear it. Now, get started on your work, please."

Helena banged around, setting out brushes and paints. She then rose and swept to the back of the class to fill a jam jar at the sink.

"Thanks for nothing!" she hissed as she passed Kirsten.

"What? I didn't do anything!"

"You deliberately yelled out, so Miss Strong saw me flicking pellets! I bet

you just loved getting me into trouble,"
Helena accused.

Kirsten didn't reply. She was too upset
to notice Storm's furry brow dipping in a
frown.

Helena turned the tap and filled the
jam jar to the brim. As she sauntered
back past Kirsten's desk, Helena
pretended to trip. Her arm shot out as
she "accidentally" chucked water all over
Kirsten's sunflower picture.

"Oops. Clumsy me!"

Kirsten gasped. "Oh no! My painting.
It's ruined!"

Helena smirked. "Aw! How sad!"

"You did that on purpose!" Kirsten
cried, jumping to her feet.

Suddenly, she felt a strange prickling

sensation flow down her spine as huge golden sparks ignited in Storm's shaggy, light brown fur and his low-set ears crackled and fizzed with magical power.

Something very strange was about to happen.

Chapter
FIVE

Storm's bright midnight blue eyes glowed
as he lifted a tiny light brown front paw
and aimed a big *whoosh* of swirling glitter
at Kirsten's flooded desk.

Kirsten watched in complete astonishment
as the magical glitter flashed around,
vacuuming up the spilled water. Water
droplets began rising upward from her
picture, like rain falling in reverse. In
seconds, her picture was as good as new.

All the water now formed a giant,
shining teardrop. Storm waved his paw

again and, just as if someone had pressed fast forward, the water shot sideways and whizzed toward Helena, who had now turned her back.

But Storm's aim was slightly off. The giant teardrop missed Helena by an inch. *Splosh!* It smacked straight into Tracy and burst, drenching the front of her school sweater.

Tracy screeched in shock and leaped to her feet. "What did you do that for?"

"It wasn't me . . . I mean . . . er . . . it was an accident," Kirsten stammered. She could hardly explain that her invisible puppy friend was the culprit. Even if she had, Tracy wouldn't have believed her. "Um . . . Sorry," she finished lamely.

Helena grabbed a handful of paper towels and started dabbing at Tracy's sweater. "Kirsten just did that on purpose. She's jealous because you want to be friends with me and not only with her!"

"I am not!" Kirsten fumed. Even if she did feel a bit hurt, she certainly wouldn't have taken it out on Tracy. "Tracy can be friends with whoever she likes!"

"Tracy knows that. It's not like she

needs *your* permission!" Helena shot back at her.

"That's enough!" Miss Strong stood there with her hands on her hips. "What's gotten into you three today? You're like wild animals! Tracy, go into the coatroom and get changed. Helena, go back to your seat. And Kirsten, get back to your work."

"But, Miss . . ." Helena began.

"Now, if you please," Miss Strong said firmly.

Helena slunk off and sat down, while Tracy went toward the coatroom.

Kirsten stood there for a moment longer, still amazed by how quickly the argument had broken out. She was tempted to tell the teacher that Helena had started it. But she'd never been a tattletale and she wasn't about to start being one now, however infuriating Helena was.

As Kirsten slowly sank onto her chair, Storm climbed into her lap. "I am sorry. I seem to have made things worse for you," he whined softly.

"That's all right. You were just trying to help," Kirsten whispered.

She was dying to give Storm a big
cuddle to show that she wasn't angry
with him, but she didn't dare risk it
with Helena still glaring at her across the
room. She had to settle for just patting
him.

"I'm going to the tennis club. Do you
want a ride to the gym?" Mr. Blake
asked, after Kirsten had helped clear the
dishes after dinner that night.

"That would be great," Kirsten said.
She thought about calling Tracy and
asking if she wanted to be picked up.
But Tracy hadn't spoken to her since
the soaking incident in art class. Kirsten
decided that it might be better to wait
and try to talk to her during practice.

Clearing the air between them might be easier without Helena around.

Kirsten sat in the back of the car with Storm on her lap as her dad drove to the gym. "You won't have to be invisible at the gym," Kirsten whispered. "I'm sure Molly won't mind me bringing you, as long as she sees that you're really well behaved."

Storm nodded.

As the car pulled up, Kirsten got out with Storm in her arms. "Thanks for the ride. See you later, Dad," she said, waving as he drove off.

Kirsten and Storm went inside with some other girls who had just arrived. They all crowded around and wanted to know about Storm. Molly was getting changed into some tracksuit bottoms. She looked up as Kirsten, Storm, and the other girls came into the changing room.

"What's all the commotion? Oh, what an adorable puppy," Molly said as a big smile spread across her face. "What's his name?"

"Storm," Kirsten told her. "I haven't had him long, but I love him to pieces."

"Who wouldn't love him?" said one of the girls stroking Storm. "He's so cute!"

"Enough of the fussing already! Go get changed," Molly said. She looked thoughtful. "It's about time the Limelight Majorettes had a mascot. A puppy like Storm would be perfect. But he'd have to be well-trained. I suppose Storm is too young, Kirsten?"

"No, no! Storm could do it," Kirsten exclaimed. "I've . . . er . . . been encouraging him to march with me when I practice baton twirling at home."

"Well, if that's so, I'd love to see him doing it. Do you think you can show us before practice starts? We're still waiting for a few girls to arrive," Molly said.

"Um . . . Right now?" Kirsten said.

She hadn't banked on an instant demonstration and started to regret her impulsive outburst. "I'll just ask St—I mean, I'll just get Storm ready. He . . . er . . . has to get into the mood."

"Fine," Molly said. "Come on, everyone. Let's leave Kirsten and Storm to it." She ushered the other girls out of the changing room.

The moment they were alone, Kirsten sank onto a bench. "Oh heck. Now what am I going to do? I'm sorry, Storm. I should have asked if you wanted to be our mascot. We can forget the whole idea. I'll think up some excuse to tell Molly."

"Wait, Kirsten," Storm yapped, his

large, midnight blue eyes glinting. "What would I have to do?"

"Well, you'd have to wear a little uniform in the group's colors and walk beside me as I march in the parade. Mascots are supposed to bring good luck," Kirsten explained.

Storm showed his sharp little teeth in a grin. "That sounds good. I would like to try!"

"You would? That's amazing!" Kirsten said delightedly. She quickly pulled on her T-shirt and short pleated skirt. "Now we have to convince Molly that you're the right puppy for the job. I'll talk you through the routine as I do it. Okay?"

As Kirsten returned to the gym with Storm, she could feel her palms sweating.

Despite the little puppy's eagerness, she was really nervous about messing up in front of everyone.

The door opened as more girls arrived for practice. Kirsten saw Tracy come in. Helena was just behind her.

Kirsten groaned inwardly. That's all she needed.

"Quiet, please, everyone," Molly called out. "Ready, Kirsten?" she said, placing a CD into the player.

Kirsten felt her face growing hot, but she forced herself to concentrate. She struck a pose and smiled encouragingly at Storm. He was looking up at her with his ears pricked, awaiting instructions.

As the intro music rang out, Kirsten began the routine. "Okay, forward, left wheel. Follow me . . ." she instructed Storm.

Storm lifted his chin, picked up his paws and marched confidently beside her.

Kirsten's baton flashed as she twirled it expertly, while high-stepping in time to the music. Storm followed her every word and wheeled back and forth as she did the complicated routine.

As the music faded, Kirsten stopped. Beside her, Storm stretched out one front paw and dipped his head in a bow.

A chorus of cheers rang out, followed by a burst of applause. Kirsten was shocked to see that even Tracy and Helena were clapping enthusiastically.

Molly came over to congratulate her. "You were right, Kirsten. Storm will be a wonderful mascot for us. We'll have to see about getting him a uniform. Do you think you'll be able to bring him to practice regularly, so that he can get used to marching with the whole troupe?"

Kirsten glanced across at Storm, who

was rolling on his back so that he could have his tummy rubbed by two majorettes. "I think I might have trouble actually keeping him away!"

Chapter
SIX

As Tracy came over, Kirsten prepared herself to apologize again for soaking her in class earlier.

But her friend seemed to have forgotten all about it. She bent down to pet Storm. "Hello, boy. Aren't you cute?" She looked up at Kirsten. "Is he one of the strays your mom and dad are always trying to find homes for?"

Kirsten nodded, and spotted Helena wandering over to join them. "He's a new one. Storm's a really special little

pup." She smiled secretly to herself, imagining the look on Tracy's face if she could have known how special Storm *really* was. "I'm hoping Mom will let me keep him. I'm waiting for the right time to ask her."

"I wouldn't mind having a new puppy," Helena said wistfully. "But my mom doesn't like pets. She says they're messy and taking care of them takes up too much time."

"That's a shame," Kirsten said. "I couldn't imagine not having a pet."

"You're really lucky to be able to take care of all kinds of different puppies," Helena went on. "What kind is Storm? Is he a mutt?"

Kirsten smiled. "No. But I wouldn't mind if he was. He's a Border terrier."

"I've never heard of those," Helena said, looking interested. "Are they rare?"

"I'm not sure. You'd have to ask my mom. She's the expert," Kirsten said. *Helena seems to like puppies almost as much as I do*, she thought with surprise.

Helena bent down to stroke Storm. "Hello, little fella!"

At first Storm eyed Helena warily but then he allowed her to pat him and began slowly wagging his tail. Kirsten noticed that Storm seemed to be slightly warming toward Helena.

"I guess we really should do some work," Kirsten said eventually to Tracy as Helena stood up again.

Tracy nodded. "Will you be okay by yourself, Helena?"

"I'll be fine watching. Can I watch Storm, if he's not practicing with you all the time?" Helena said.

Kirsten was about to say that Storm didn't need looking after, but when she glanced at him, he gave a small woof of agreement.

"Sure. Why not," Kirsten said

generously. Storm was with her all day. It wouldn't hurt for Helena to share him for a few minutes.

The rest of practice went well. Tracy worked hard, earning herself some praise from Molly, and Storm followed all the routines perfectly. Kirsten noticed that Helena was sitting watching everything closely. She was unusually quiet.

Mr. Blake called in just as practice ended. He was passing the gym and wondered if Kirsten and Storm wanted a ride home.

"Can we take Tracy and Helena, too?" Kirsten asked, deciding to try not to be so suspicious of Helena all the time.

They all piled into the car. Helena sat in the backseat with Tracy. "I didn't know being a majorette was so complicated. You have to do millions of warm-ups and stretches and leg-strengthening stuff. It's like you're real athletes."

Kirsten glanced at her in the rearview mirror. "We are! You have to be really in shape to do the routines."

"Dad's always telling me I should do some sports. I think I might ask Molly

about joining," Helena mused.

Kirsten raised her eyebrows. She was starting not to mind Helena so much. But she still wasn't sure if she liked the idea of her joining in with everything that she and Tracy did together. She decided not to say anything just now.

When Mr. Blake stopped outside Tracy's house, Tracy and Helena both got out.

"Thanks for the ride," they chorused.

"See you in the morning," Tracy called.

"Bye!" Kirsten waved.

Once they got home, Kirsten asked her mom and dad if they'd like some hot chocolate. She spooned chocolate powder into three mugs. While she was waiting for the teapot to boil, she rummaged in a cabinet and found a tasty, bone-shaped dog chew for Storm.

"Here you go. You deserve a yummy treat. I was so proud of you at practice," she told him.

"I enjoyed being a mascot," Storm yapped.

He bounced forward onto his short front legs and grabbed the chew. Picking it up, he trotted around the kitchen with both ends of it sticking out of his mouth.

Kirsten made the drinks and put them on a tray. She laughed as Storm followed her into the sitting room with his prize. "You'd better sit on your old blanket to eat that or Mom'll go nuts!" she whispered.

★

Kirsten jogged across the school playing field a few mornings later with Storm trotting along invisibly beside her.

Miss Strong was already on the hockey field handing out yellow and green sashes and organizing the class into teams. Kirsten was in the Greens and Tracy and Helena were in the Yellows.

"Kirsten and Tracy, you're center forwards, so you'll face off for the ball." Miss Strong looked around, checking that everyone was in position.

Kirsten flexed her knees as she faced Tracy on the center line.

Storm began leaping around her ankles excitedly. "Tell me what to do and I will follow you, Kirsten!" he yapped so that only Kirsten heard him.

With a tingle of alarm, it dawned on Kirsten that Storm thought playing field hockey was like a majorette routine. He didn't realize that he could be kicked by a player or hit by a hockey stick. She couldn't warn him of the danger with everyone so close.

Miss Strong picked up the whistle

dangling by a cord around her neck.

Phee-eep! The game was on.

Kirsten won the face-off. She ran down the field, hoping to get away from the other players. Once she was out of earshot, she'd be able to tell Storm to get off the field.

Storm gave a joyful bark and dashed after Kirsten, his strong little legs eating up the grass. Kirsten glanced sideways at him as she ran with the ball, but Helena was pounding after her and she still couldn't warn Storm of the danger.

"To me, Kirsten!" one of the players cried.

"Come on, Yellows. Tackle her!"

Helena dodged forward. She tackled Kirsten and won the ball. Lifting her stick, Helena swiveled, about to send the ball out to a winger.

Kirsten gasped with horror as Storm dashed forward and stood in front of Helena. He was right in the path of the rock-hard hockey ball.

Chapter
SEVEN

"Look out!" Quick as a flash, Kirsten dropped her stick and shoved against Helena with her whole body.

"Oh!" Helena skidded and only just managed to stop herself from falling over. Her hockey stick slammed down, missing the ball.

Pheep! Miss Strong blew the whistle for a foul as she ran toward them. "I saw that, Kirsten! You did it deliberately. I will not tolerate this behavior. Go and get changed and wait for me in the classroom."

Helena stood there with a hurt

expression on her face. She looked more
upset than angry.

Kirsten felt terrible, but at least Storm
was uninjured. Her shoulders drooped as
she trailed across the field.

Tracy jogged up to her. "What
happened? I thought you were starting to
like Helena."

"I was . . . I am . . ." Kirsten said.

"Well, you've got a funny way of showing it!"

"I wasn't *trying* to hurt Helena, honest!" Kirsten protested. "But I couldn't help it—" She stopped. There was nothing else she could say without giving away Storm's secret. "I can't explain. But you have to believe me."

Tracy looked puzzled. "I don't know, Kirsten . . ."

Sighing heavily, Kirsten left the field and headed for the changing rooms.

Storm bounded after her. "Thank you for saving me, Kirsten," he panted. "But now you are in even more trouble because of me."

"I'll live with it," Kirsten said

resignedly. "It's more important that you're okay. It was my fault, anyway. I should have warned you to stay off the hockey field. Don't worry, Miss Strong will probably make me write out a hundred lines or clean the art cabinet. It's no big deal."

But the teacher decided on a more serious punishment.

"Detention!" Kirsten cried, gaping at her. "But I *can't* stay behind after school, Miss. I've got majorette practice."

"I'm afraid you should have thought of that earlier," Miss Strong said firmly, adjusting her glasses—today they were bright red. "I'll let your parents know that you'll be home late."

At the end of the day's lessons, Kirsten

sat with her chin propped in her hands as
everyone filed out of class.

"Bad luck," Helena said as she passed
Kirsten's desk. "No hard feelings, eh?"
And for once, she sounded as if she
meant it.

"Thanks," Kirsten said, managing
a half-smile. Helena was being really
fair about this and Kirsten realized that
she'd stopped minding so much about
Helena becoming best friends with her
and Tracy. Maybe it could work—if *she*
hadn't now messed things up.

Miss Strong picked up a pile of papers from her desk. "I have a few things to do in the staff room. I won't be long. Continue working on your art project, please." She went out and closed the classroom door behind her.

Kirsten groaned. "Now what am I going to do? I can't afford to miss practice. There're only a few left before the town parade."

Storm's furry face lit up. "I have an idea!"

Kirsten felt a familiar prickling sensation down her spine as bright gold sparks danced in Storm's shaggy, light brown fur and his bristly whiskers glowed with electricity.

There was a bright flash and a silent

explosion of sparks. *Pop!* Kirsten's CD
player appeared out of thin air and
floated on to the floor. *Crack!* Her baton
clattered down beside the CD player.
Rustle! Her school uniform was magically
transformed into a T-shirt, a short pleated
skirt, and sneakers.

Kirsten beamed at her tiny friend.
"Thanks, Storm. You're amazing!"

She switched on the CD player at a
low volume so no one would overhear,
and the intro music softly started. For the
next twenty minutes or so, Kirsten and
Storm marched up and down and around
the empty classroom. The tiny puppy
knew the routine now and Kirsten hardly
needed to tell him what to do.

"That was great," Kirsten puffed,

flexing her fingers after all the baton twirling. "I can't wait until we're marching in the real parade! Let's do one more run-through before Miss Strong comes back."

Storm suddenly froze and his ears twitched. "I think she is coming now!"

Waving a paw, he sent another spray of golden sparks through the air. *Crackle!* The CD player and baton disappeared

instantly and Kirsten was, once again, wearing her school uniform.

As the classroom door began to open, Kirsten realized that she was nowhere near her desk where she was supposed to be working on her project. "Uh-oh, Miss Strong's going to go bananas. I'll probably get triple detention now!"

There was a sudden mega-*whoosh* of movement and Kirsten felt herself flying through the air.

"Oof!" She landed in her chair with a bump.

She was only just in time. Miss Strong's small, neat figure appeared in the doorway.

"You can clean up your things and go now, Kirsten. I think I've made my point. Let's have no more of this silly behavior. It's just not like you."

"No, Miss. Thanks," Kirsten said in a subdued voice.

Storm had a mischievous look on his face. He had obviously really enjoyed their practice session and was disappointed that it had been cut short. Leaping up to balance on his back legs, he began pirouetting toward the door.

A big bubble of laughter threatened to burst from Kirsten's lips. She stuffed her work into her school bag and ran into the hallway.

C h a p t e r
EIGHT

Luckily Kirsten's mom and dad weren't too annoyed with her for getting detention and accepted her explanation that it was all a mistake.

"You don't have a mean bone in your body, Kirsten Blake," her dad said. "Even if you do have a one-track mind about being in the majorettes!"

"Me?" Kirsten made her eyes all big. "I don't know what you mean," she joked.

They all laughed as they settled down to dinner.

Kirsten's mom spotted Storm sitting beside Kirsten's chair. She shook her head. "You know I can never find that puppy when you're at school. He doesn't come out of hiding, however much I call him or waft a dish of food around. But it's amazing how he always appears the second you come home."

"Amazing," Kirsten echoed innocently, around a mouthful of macaroni and cheese.

A couple of evenings later, Molly called. She wanted Storm's measurements for his costume. Kirsten said she'd get them and then call her back.

As soon as she'd hung up, Kirsten searched out her mom's tape measure. She lifted Storm up onto a table and then looped the tape around his compact little body.

Storm wagged his tail and tried to twist around to lick her face.

"Hey! Stop wriggling! This is like a juggling act!" Kirsten was struggling to hold the ends of the tape together with one hand while jotting figures on to a piece of paper with the other.

Finally it was done. "I'll give these measurements to Molly. I can't wait to see your costume!"

On the following Saturday afternoon, Kirsten decided to take Storm for a walk before meeting up with Tracy and Helena at a row of stores along the main road. A new fast food place called Smoothers had just opened. They had planned to have a milkshake with their allowance money before going to practice.

"I don't mind about Helena joining the Limelight Majorettes," Kirsten told Storm. "I thought she'd just come along to mess around, but she seems serious about it. I heard Molly saying that she thinks Helena's going to be really good."

"I am glad that you are good friends with Helena now," Storm woofed.

We're almost there, Kirsten thought, a small smile on her face.

Kirsten said her good-byes to her parents and then she and Storm set off. They headed to a short alleyway that led to a field at the back of some houses. The fences of all the backyards backed on to the field.

Storm sniffed around in the grass, seeking out interesting smells and then raced around enjoying himself. He found a muddy twig and held it in his little front paws to chew one end.

Suddenly, Kirsten heard loud growling and barking coming from behind one of the wooden fences. A noise like scratching claws filled the air as the unseen dogs tried to get into the field.

Storm yelped and dropped the twig. He rushed over to Kirsten and crouched beside her, trembling from head to foot.

"What's wrong? Have you hurt your mouth on that wood?" Kirsten said worriedly. She picked him up and cradled him in her arms.

Storm's midnight blue eyes widened in

terror. "Shadow knows where I am. He has used his magic on those dogs. They are trying to get to me."

Kirsten's heart missed a beat as she realized that her friend was in great danger. Her mind whirled as she tried to think of the best thing to do. "That's a pretty high fence. I don't think they can get over," she judged. "But you'd better hide in my bag, just in case. We're leaving, right now!"

Kirsten opened her shoulder bag and tucked the terrified puppy inside. Storm immediately curled up into a tight ball and lay there shaking.

Her pulse racing, Kirsten jogged back toward the alleyway. She clutched her bag tightly so that Storm wasn't jostled around too much.

"I hope we don't meet any more of Shadow's dogs. How will I be able to tell if they're dangerous?" Kirsten asked nervously.

"They will have cruel, pale eyes and extra long teeth." Storm's muffled woof rose from her bag.

Once she was back out on the street, Kirsten gradually slowed down. No fierce dogs had run after them and the growling and snarling grew faint and then stopped altogether.

"I think they've given up," she puffed, feeling weak with relief.

Storm uncurled and cautiously peered out of the unzipped bag. He tensed as he listened hard and then his whole body relaxed. "You are right, Kirsten. I am safe for the moment. But if Shadow finds me again, I may have to leave suddenly, without saying good-bye."

Kirsten experienced a sharp pang at the thought of losing her friend. She knew that she would never be ready to let him go. "I hope that evil Shadow never finds you and then you can stay with me forever!"

Storm twisted to look up at her with serious midnight blue eyes. "I cannot do that. One day I must return to my own world to lead the Moon-claw pack."

"I know," Kirsten said in a small voice, but she didn't really want to think about it. She was determined to enjoy every single moment with her magical friend. She tried changing the subject.

"I bet Tracy and Helena are already at Smoothers. Let's go and meet them."

Storm sat up and rested his front paws outside the shoulder bag as Kirsten turned onto the busy main road. A bit farther on, she saw Tracy and Helena on the opposite side of the road. They were just passing a video store.

They spotted her, too, and waved.

Kirsten walked toward a pedestrian crosswalk in front of a building with scaffolding covering it. A clanging noise came from high up where builders were at work.

As Kirsten went to press the button to cross, there was a shout.

"Look out below!" someone warned.

Kirsten glanced behind her and looked up. A heavy bucket clanged onto one of the scaffolding boards and then came tumbling downward. It was heading straight for her and Storm.

Kirsten froze. Her legs turned to water as she gathered herself for a painful collision.

But familiar bright sparks glittered in Storm's shaggy fur and a huge spray of gold sparks shot upward. The bucket faltered as if Kirsten had pressed slow motion on a TV remote. A fine dusting of sparks drifted down to settle on Kirsten and weird rippling feelings ran up the ends of her fingers and toes and zipped through her body.

There was a sudden jolt as the bucket crashed down on top of her and Storm.

Kirsten gasped as it passed *right through* her. She felt a slurpy sensation, like jelly wobbling, and a sucking *plop!* as the heavy bucket clanged onto the pavement and bounced away harmlessly.

She heard running steps. Two builders emerged from inside the building, looking white-faced.

"Thank goodness. It just missed her!" one of them said shakily.

The other one picked up the bucket. He scratched his head. "How the blazes . . . You sure you're all right?"

Kirsten quickly gathered her wits. "I'm fine. No problem. Got to go!" As the green man flashed up on the crosswalk sign, Kirsten hurried across the road. "Phew! That was close! Thanks, Storm," she whispered.

"You are welcome," Storm barked.

Helena and Tracy were hurrying along the pavement to meet them. "What just happened? We heard shouting and a massive crash," Tracy said.

"Was there an accident?" Helena asked worriedly.

"Nah! It was no big deal. Just two builders making lots of noise," Kirsten said. Her face lit up with mischief. She stepped quickly around Tracy and began sprinting toward the shops. "Last one inside Smoothers pays for the milkshakes!"

"You're on!" her friends yelled.

Chapter

NINE

Storm marched back and forth, proudly high-stepping around the gym. His tiny red top hat leaned at an angle, covering one ear. A sparkling red jacket with shiny gold epaulettes and matching buttons reached halfway down his body.

Tracy wore her dress uniform of a pleated skirt and a cute red jacket, trimmed with gold braid. A red plumed top hat and knee-length gold boots completed her outfit.

The Limelight Majorettes were having

a full dress rehearsal. There was one day left before the town parade. Tracy and Helena, and the other members of the B team, stood watching everyone marching and twirling batons.

"Way to go, Kirsten! Storm's doing great!" Tracy called out encouragingly, clapping in time to the music. Although she was trying to smile and look happy, there was a wistful expression on her face.

Kirsten knew her friend must be

longing to take part. She noticed that Molly looked thoughtful. When everyone stopped for a break, Kirsten saw the trainer take Tracy aside and have a word with her.

"I think Molly might be going to give Tracy a second chance!" she whispered to Storm.

Storm wagged his tail. "I think so, too."

"Yay!" Tracy suddenly cheered and punched the air before hurtling toward the changing rooms. "I'm on the A team," she sang out.

Everyone clapped, including Helena. Kirsten had a big grin on her face. She picked Storm up and whirled around with him in a little dance of happiness.

Storm's tail twirled madly and he yapped with delight.

A few minutes later, Tracy reappeared, resplendent in full dress uniform, and proudly took her place in the ranks next to Kirsten.

"Wow!" Helena shrieked, jumping up and down. "Watch out, Kirsten. Watch out, Tracy. I'll be marching beside you next year."

Kirsten looked toward her and smiled, her eyes glowing. "I really hope so!" she called out.

The day of the parade dawned bright and clear.

Kirsten woke early. Two uniforms were hanging from a hook on her bedroom door. She leaped out of bed, too excited to go back to sleep.

"Come on, Storm. We might as well start getting ready."

Kirsten washed quickly and dragged a brush through her hair and then decided to give Storm a brush. He gave her a

pained doggy grin and managed to put up with it for about half a minute before he started play-growling and trying to bite the brush.

Kirsten giggled. "I get the message!"

Ten minutes later, she and Storm stood side by side, looking in her wardrobe mirror. "Don't we look great?" Kirsten said admiringly.

She was too excited to eat breakfast and only managed a mouthful of toast. Her mom drove the short distance into town. As Kirsten, Storm, and her parents emerged from the garage, Kirsten saw Molly and the others at the meeting point on the market square.

"See you later," she said to her mom and dad, hurrying toward the LMs.

Tracy was already there and Helena was just arriving with her parents. She waved to Kirsten and Storm. "Good luck. Knock 'em dead!" she cried.

Kirsten took a deep breath. "This is it. Ready?" she whispered to Storm.

Storm nodded, holding his head high.

The Limelight Majorettes took their positions. The brass band began to play.

Sunlight glinted off the polished buttons and musical instruments.

Kirsten, Storm, Tracy, and the rest of the majorettes moved forward.

The crowds cheered as the parade progressed through the streets. Colored banners fluttered from the stalls and smells of cotton candy and burgers filled the air. Entertainers juggled clubs, and acrobats tumbled through the air.

Kirsten twirled her baton, high-stepping
in perfect time to the cheerful beat.
Beside her, Storm's red hat nodded as he
marched at heel.

The colorful parade moved through
the streets. It seemed like no time at all
to Kirsten before the majorettes and the
band came to a halt. The mayor, wearing
her gold chain over a pretty blue suit, cut
the ribbon and declared the new store
open.

"Great job, everyone," Molly said,
beaming at her troupe. "And well
done, Storm. You're a perfect mascot. I
suggest you all relax now and enjoy the
entertainment."

The delicious smells of food had made

Kirsten hungry. She decided to buy a burger and share it with Storm. But as she went to speak to him, he suddenly whimpered and tore away through the crowd.

Kirsten didn't hesitate. She ran after him and just glimpsed him running into a loading dock at the rear of a store. She whipped around at the familiar sound of growling and saw two large dogs some distance away. They were sniffing around under some parked vans.

A cold shiver ran down Kirsten's back as she saw their pale eyes and long sharp teeth.

Storm was in terrible danger.

Kirsten rushed into the loading dock and slipped down between two parked

trucks. Suddenly, there was a dazzling flash of bright gold light and sparks sprayed in all directions.

Kirsten saw Storm, a tiny helpless puppy no longer, but a magnificent, young, silver-gray wolf. His thick neck-ruff looked as if it had been sprinkled with a thousand tiny gold diamonds. An older wolf with a gentle face stood beside Storm.

And then Kirsten knew that her friend was leaving. Her throat tightened with tears, but she knew she would have to be strong for Storm's sake.

"Quick, Storm. Your enemies are near. Save yourself," she urged.

Storm's big, midnight blue eyes softened with affection. "You have been a true friend, Kirsten. Be of good heart."

She rushed forward and threw her arms around Storm's muscular neck. "I'm really going to miss you," she sobbed, her voice breaking.

Storm allowed her to hug him. He held up one huge, silvery paw as a final burst of bright gold light filled the loading dock and sparks crackled down around Kirsten and went out as they hit the floor.

The two wolves faded and were gone.

On the floor by Kirsten's feet lay something red and gold. Storm's tiny mascot uniform. A deep sadness swept through her, only made better by the relief at knowing that Storm was safe. She would never forget her wonderful friend and would always treasure the memories of their time together.

Kirsten heard a final fierce growl from behind her and then there was silence. She whirled around just in time to see two normal-looking dogs slinking away.

"Kirsten?" called a voice. Helena stood at the entrance to the loading dock. She was holding a tiny puppy with shaggy, light brown fur. "I just found Storm running around outside. I don't know how he got out of his uniform," she said.

Kirsten did a double take. "But that's not St—" Kirsten stopped as the strangest feeling came over her.

An image of Storm's mischievous face popped into her mind and then a knowing smile crept over Kirsten's face.

She gazed at the tiny puppy that looked just like Storm in almost every way. Only she would ever know that this wasn't Storm.

As the tiny, lost puppy looked at her with frightened, brownish blue eyes, Kirsten knew exactly what she had to do. "*Storm*. Look at you running off like that," she pretended to scold as she took the tiny puppy from Helena. "I'll have to take really good care of you from now on!"

About the Author

Sue Bentley's books for children often include animals or fairies. She lives in Northampton and enjoys reading, going to the movies, and sitting watching the frogs and newts in her garden pond. If she hadn't been a writer, she would probably have been a skydiver or a brain surgeon. The main reason she writes is that she can drink pots and pots of tea while she's typing. She has met and owned many cats and dogs and each one has brought a special kind of magic to her life.

Magic Puppy

Read all of the other books
in the Magic Puppy series!

#1 A New Beginning

#2 Muddy Paws

#3 Cloud Capers

#4 Star of the Show

#5 Party Dreams

#6 A Forest Charm

#7 Twirling Tails

#8 School of Mischief